Hee-Haw-Dini AND the GREAT ZAMBINI

Kim Kennedy

Illustrated by Doug Kennedy

Abrams Books for Young Readers ✳ New York

On a farm there lived a little donkey named Hee-Haw. His best friend was a field mouse named Chester. They loved to sit under an apple tree and practice magic tricks.

"One day," Hee-Haw would say, "we will become real magicians. We will travel to exciting places and do amazing things!"

"Just like the Great Zambini, the world's most famous magician!" Chester would chime in.

The other farm animals would just shake their heads, but still Hee-Haw and Chester practiced, day after day, under the apple tree.

One morning, Rabbit passed by while Hee-Haw and Chester were trying out some new tricks.

"Would you like me to pull you from this hat?" Hee-Haw asked Rabbit.

"I'll believe it when I see it!" laughed Rabbit, hopping away.

Along came Goose and Pig.

"Would you like to see me make an egg disappear?" asked Hee-Haw.

"No," honked Goose.

"Then allow me to pull a coin from your ear," squeaked Chester.

"Nope," grunted Pig.

"Don't you think it's time the two of you quit practicing magic tricks?" Goose snapped. "Everyone knows that there is no way farm animals from the country could ever be magicians."

Chester sighed.

"Don't listen to them," Hee-Haw told Chester. "They obviously don't know about the Magician's Secret Motto."

"You're right," said Chester, reciting the motto: "In order to become a magician, one must believe that magical things can happen."

Suddenly, Hee-Haw's big ears twitched, hearing the whistle of a locomotive. "Look!" he said. "A circus train is coming!"

One by one, the boxcars passed. Each was grand, but the last was the most spectacular of all.

It belonged to the Great Zambini!

After the train had faded from sight, Hee-Haw noticed something lying in the grass.

"It's the Great Zambini's magic chest," he said. "It must have fallen from the train." Hee-Haw snuck the trunk back to his stall.

"Let's open it," whispered Hee-Haw.

"How?" asked Chester. "We don't have a key."

"This calls for the *unlock-o-maneuver*," said Hee-Haw, trying his skills on the lock. Then he waved his hooves slowly above the chest.

"Open sesame," he commanded. With a **CLICK**, the shimmering lid opened.

"Wow!" the friends said, gazing inside.

All night long, Hee-Haw and Chester practiced with the Great Zambini's very own cards, props, and magic wands. They read his book of magic and even learned some of his most difficult illusions.

Finally, the two were ready to do what magicians do: put on a magic show.

"We'll perform the magic show in disguise," said Hee-Haw. "Everyone will come if they believe that we are famous magicians from somewhere far away from this farm."

"Then we'll need fantastic names," said Chester. "I will be . . . Zaba Zaba the Magnificent."

"And I," said the donkey with a bow, "will be Hee-Haw-Dini!"

While the rest of the animals snoozed, Hee-Haw and
Chester hung posters around the farm.

"Did you hear?" Goose flapped the next morning. "A magic
show featuring the amazing Hee-Haw-Dini and Zaba Zaba is
going to take place in the barn tonight!"

"Oh, really?" said Hee-Haw, winking at Chester.

"Yes!" she squawked. "It's your chance to see *real*
magicians."

"We'll be there," said Hee-Haw. "You can count on that."

MAGIC SHOW
TONIGHT IN THE BARN
SEE THE
AMAZING!
HEE-HAW-DINI
AND
ZABA ZABA

There was a huge crowd that night. The barn was packed with every animal from the farm.

Their excitement kept growing until the curtains parted, revealing the mysterious Hee-Haw-Dini and Zaba Zaba. Applause filled the air as the magicians began their incredible show.

From the front row, Rabbit watched as Hee-Haw-Dini waved his wand in the air and said, "Abracadabra." In an instant, Rabbit vanished from his seat and popped out of Hee-Haw-Dini's hat.

"Now that's real magic," thought an astonished Rabbit as he searched the audience for Hee-Haw and Chester. "Where could they be?" he wondered.

"How about a volunteer?" said Hee-Haw-Dini. He plucked
Goose from the audience and cried, "Behold what magical
powers can do! Watch as this bird gets sawed in two!"

Squawks of disbelief came from the chicken section when
Goose was sawed in half and then put back together again.

"I'd like to see Hee-Haw and Chester try that!" thought Goose.

Next, Zaba Zaba pulled Pig onstage and announced, "Observe as I dare . . . to lift this very pig in the air!"

"Impossible!" shouted the crowd.

"I'll begin by summoning mysterious forces," said Zaba Zaba. "Magic-o-magic," he chanted, waving his hands around Pig. "Magic-o-magic!"

With a startled snort, Pig began to rise up, up, up, until he levitated high above the stage.

"Bravo!" the crowd cheered at the end of the show.

"I wish Hee-Haw and Chester could have been here!" blurted Goose.

"They *were* here," said Hee-Haw-Dini. Then, to everyone's surprise, the magicians removed their costumes.

"It's Hee-Haw and Chester," the crowd said with a gasp.
"I don't believe it!" cried Goose. "I don't believe it!"
"That is what makes it magic!" came a booming voice from
the shadows. It was none other than the Great Zambini himself.

"I came looking for my magic trunk, and I see that it has been put to good use," he explained. "In fact," he added, "I would like Hee-Haw and Chester to join my magic act. Together, we will travel to exciting places and do amazing things."

Goose was flabbergasted. "You would like *them* to join *you*?" she asked. "But they're just farm animals!"

"That may well be," said the Great Zambini, "but they are

also now magicians! And their greatest feat of all was making the impossible seem possible: that a donkey and a mouse could indeed become magicians."

Hee-Haw and Chester bowed as the great magician stepped onto the stage.

"Now for the grand finale," the Great Zambini announced. He raised his cape and declared:

There's more to magic than
smoke and mirrors,
or hiding a trick up your
sleeve.
True magic begins when
one has the courage
and heart to simply believe.
So bid farewell to
Zaba Zaba
and the mysterious
Hee-Haw-Dini.
The time has come for these
magical friends
to join the Great Zambini!

He swished his cape, and in a great puff of smoke . . .

They all
disappeared!

In memory of our grandmother, Anna Wollenberg Kennedy,
who had the honor of seeing Houdini perform
—K.K.

To my lovely wife, Meredith, and sons, Jackson and Julian
—D.K.

The illustrations in this book were made with acrylic paint on Arches paper.

Library of Congress Cataloging-in-Publication Data

Kennedy, Kim.
Hee-Haw-Dini and the Great Zambini / by Kim Kennedy ; illustrated by Doug Kennedy.
p. cm.
Summary: Hee-Haw the donkey and his friend Chester the field mouse long to be great magicians, and
in spite of the other farm animals' mockery, they persist in pursuing their dream.
ISBN 978-0-8109-7025-0
[1. Magicians—Fiction. 2. Magic tricks—Fiction. 3. Donkeys—Fiction. 4. Mice—Fiction. 5. Domestic
animals—Fiction.] I. Kennedy, Doug, ill. II. Title.

PZ7.K3843He 2009
[E]—dc22
2008024684

Printed and bound in China
10 9 8 7 6 5 4 3 2 1

Abrams Books for Young Readers are available at special discounts when purchased in quantity for
premiums and promotions as well as fundraising or educational use. Special editions can also be
created to specification. For details, contact specialmarkets@hnabooks.com or the address below.

HNA ▪▪▪▪▪
harry n. abrams, inc.
a subsidiary of La Martinière Groupe
115 West 18th Street
New York, NY 10011
www.hnabooks.com